The
First Fairy Tale

Book III: *Making Sense*

Written by Susan Highsmith

Illustrated by Mark Sean Wilson

Words Matter Publishing
P.O. Box 531
Salem, Il 62881
www.wordsmatterpublishing.com

ISBN 13: 978-1-949809-70-1

Library of Congress Catalog Card Number: 2020941731

Dedication

For all of us who have taken this journey ~
for all those precious ones yet to come . . .

Letter to Readers
The First Fairy Tale: Book III Making Sense

Dear Reader,

In The First Fairy Tale I: The Adventure Begins, *we met the exquisite energies that joined together in the Creation of New Life. In* Fairy Tale II: The Awakening Heart, *we greeted the dynamic forces that fashioned a beating Heart. Now, in* Fairy Tale III: Making Sense, *we journey further as this precious Being shapes itself into the individual form that will be able to leave its nurturing environment and prepare to enter an unfamiliar world.*

As you share these amazing stories with your Little One, you can recognize the power that metaphors have in soothing, healing and guiding a mind that is open and receptive to hearing about an ideal passage into Life. The developing body/ mind and emerging Spirit can benefit from hearing how much they are cherished and are acknowledged for undertaking this momentous journey.

The mind of a baby growing in your womb or resting in your arms does not require the science of what is occurring—your Little One only needs the Essence of the Love that surrounds every step of Life as it comes into Being.

Read this story in joy—enjoyment. This facet of the baby's transition from a gleam in your eye to a body in the full realization of your dream of bringing a child into your world is a glorious accomplishment. The scientific understanding of the process of gestation follows in the epilogue. The short description of development from the 22nd day to the 280th day in utero is designed to satisfy your adult mind. The epilogue provides a foundation for believing that fairy tales enhance the life of your child, even from the very beginning.

Einstein said, "If you want your children to be intelligent, read them fairy tales. If you want them to be very intelligent, read them more fairy tales." I would add here, if you want your children to feel loved, begin reading to them now, from the very first moments of their lives. It is never too soon!

Not just once but many times, and not just long ago but even now, a life begins.
In the realm of boundless splendor and infinite light a crystalline heart beats.

Within it glows three dancing lights. One is blue,
one is pink, and, in the chemistry of their union, a brilliant
yellow-gold flame shines.

Together they radiate. Both inward and outward, they gleam. The flames illuminate all the builders of form that helped this heart come into being.

11

These tiny workers continue to mold structures that will surround the heart and support its expansion.

The figure eight that cradles the heart in a tender embrace begins to extend, enfolding the fragile heart while reaching out, evolving and reflecting all life in its multiple forms.

The precious little builders gather together, curved like an apostrophe, a punctuation mark signifying connections, a sign of bringing parts together.

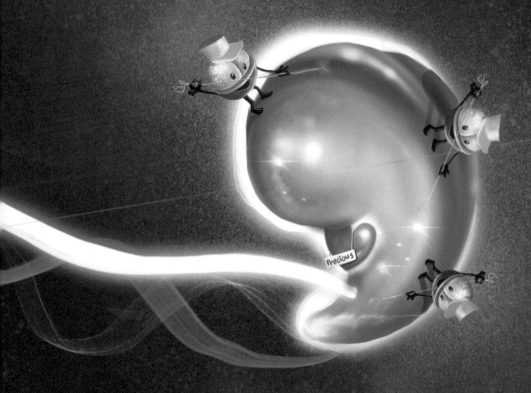

A bulb shapes itself at the top of the little body. Head to tail the arising Being is filled with all the components that will allow it to realize its potential.

19

A brain is developing. This new Being can sense, feel, and think! Special parts emerge to house its ability to act, to have emotions and thoughts. What wonders will it experience?

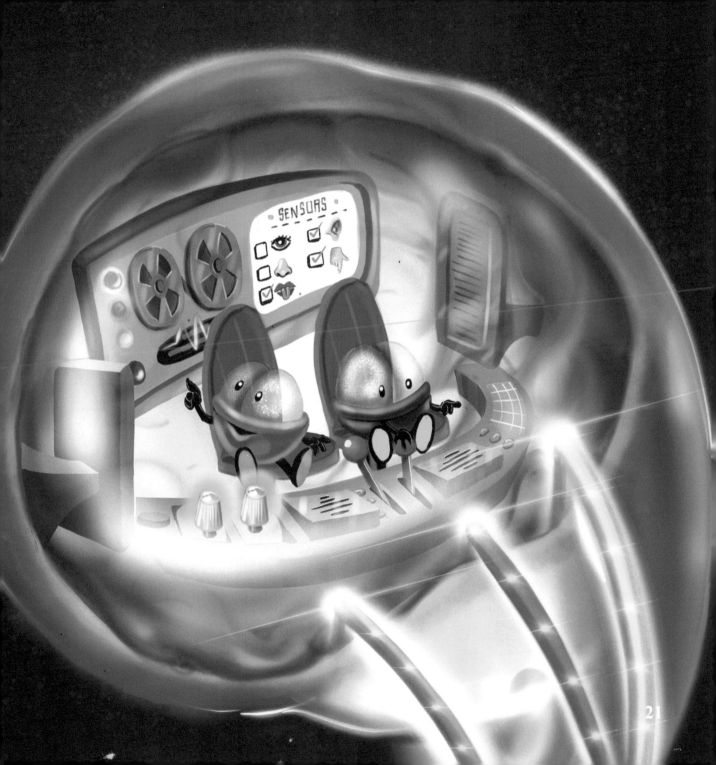

SENSORS

21

Buds begin to appear that will allow this Being to reach out, to touch and feel. Tissues within will process nutrients coming in and excess going out.

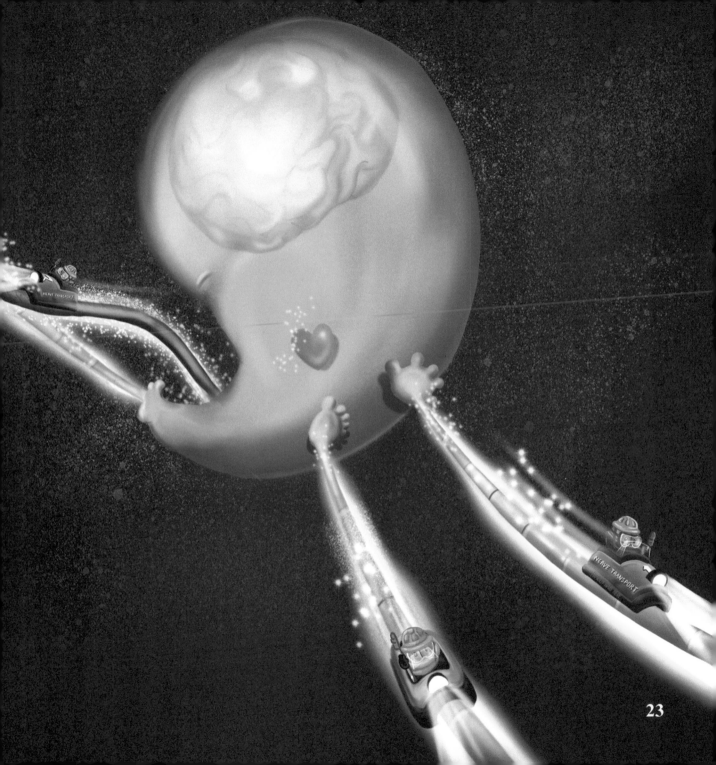

It floats and drifts and dreams in a watery environment, perfect to supply everything it needs as the monumental changes take place every instant.

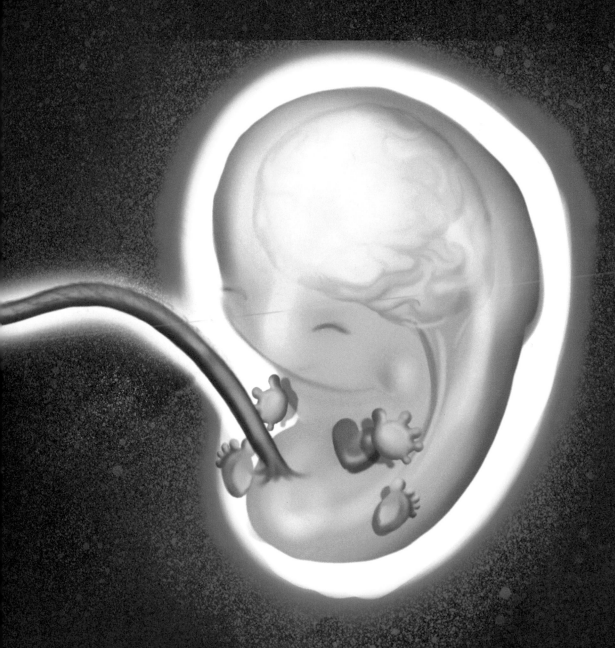

The heart continues to grow, sending out a priceless supply of energy to every creator of the beautiful form shifting and changing with each passing moment.

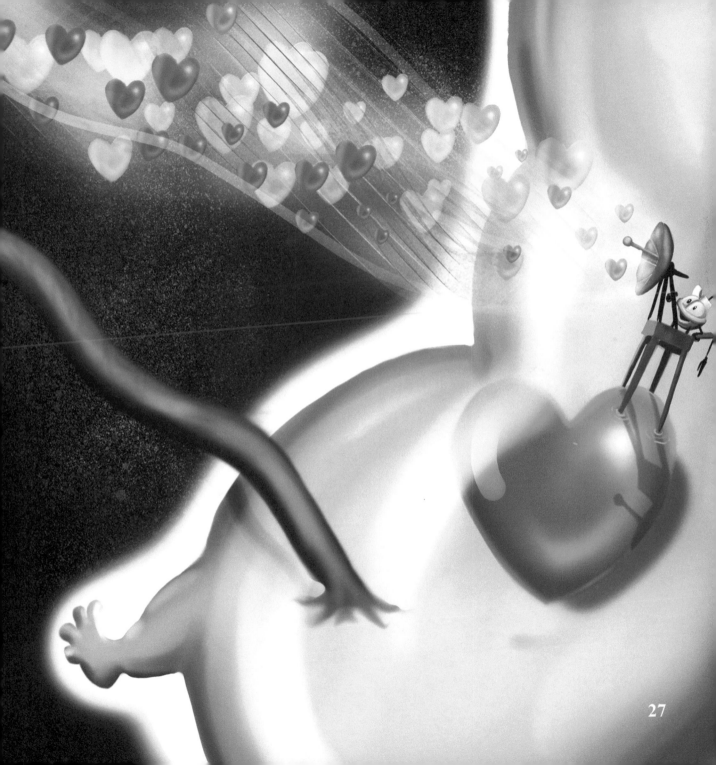

Each member of the energetic construction team is integrating into the form itself. This Little One is flourishing! It can sense in so many ways!

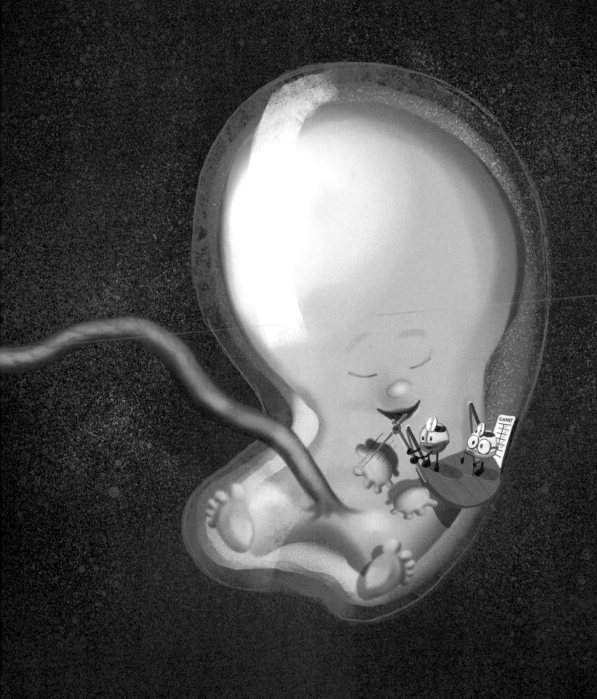

After only 14 weeks it begins to taste and smell. By 16 weeks sounds begin to be heard. Eyes have formed so this wondrous Being begins to see.

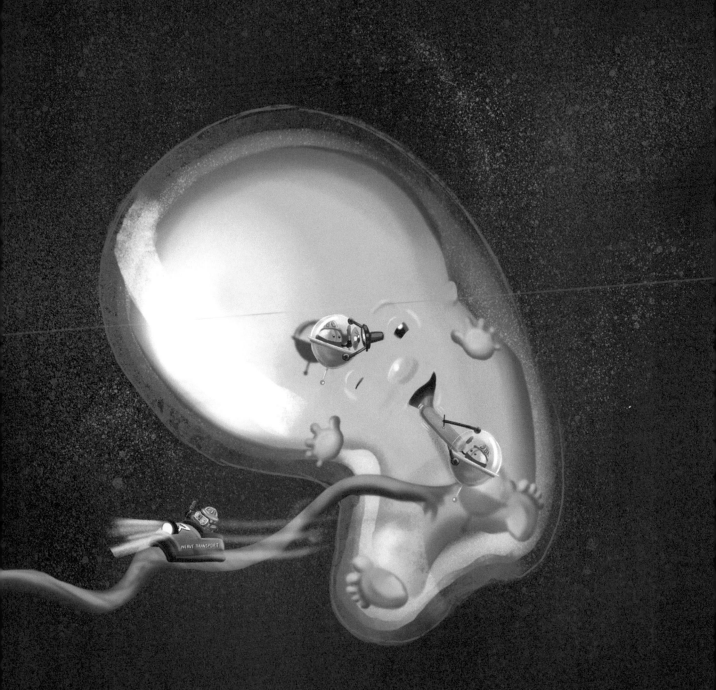

Around the crystalline heart a body has been growing. It has skin to feel, a nose to smell, a mouth to taste and speak, ears to hear, and eyes to see.

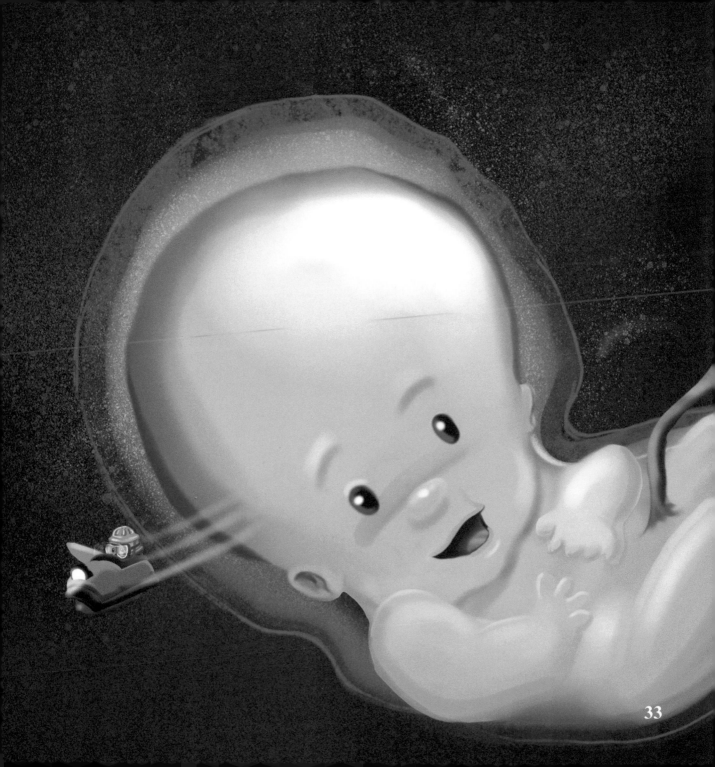

33

This Little One is preparing to emerge from the space where it has grown, and move into an entirely different world!

It is getting bigger and bigger every day! It has arms and fingers and it begins to play with a long cord that waves in front of it.

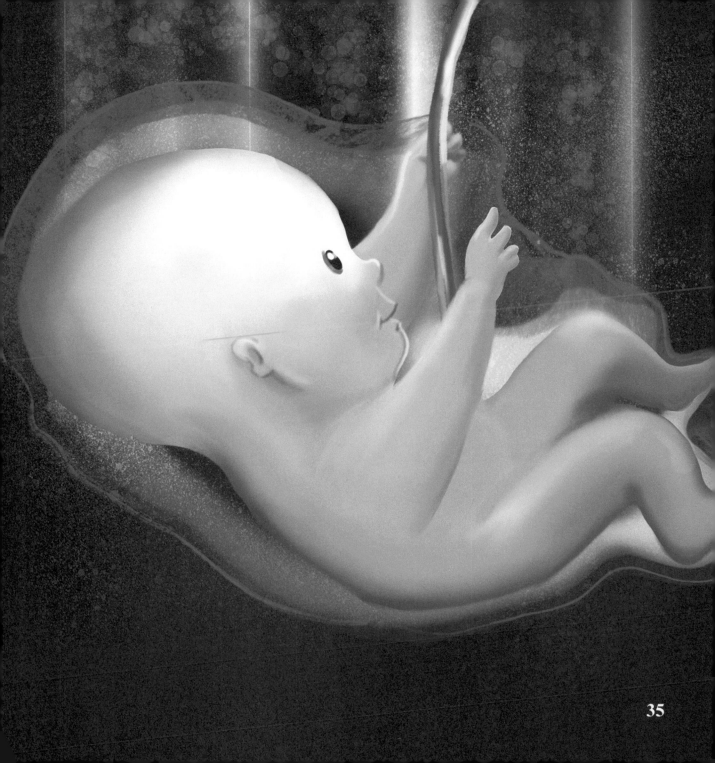

Tissues have developed that will help this beautiful Being throughout a new and different life. Each individual unit now envisions itself as part of a greater whole. The original builders now merge into organs that process, circulate, connect, distribute, respire, assimilate, eliminate—performing the most delicate tasks with ease and grace.

The builders both maintain their individuality and blend into the form itself, being absorbed into a greater and more magnificent structure, waiting, anticipating, eager to know more, be more.

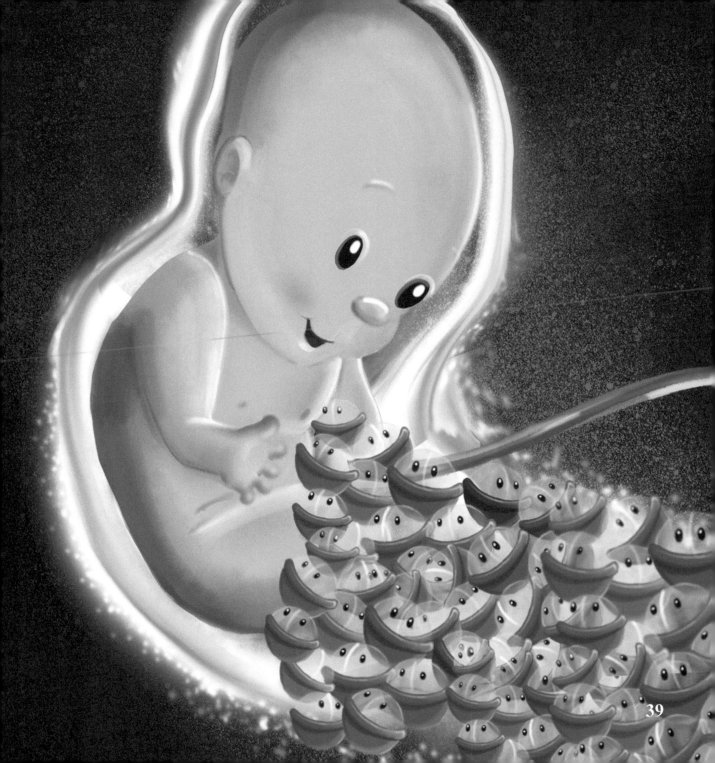

A Greater Presence watches from afar and begins to unite with this body, saying to Itself, "I see that a perfect body is taking shape. This is the garment I will wear as I sojourn through a life on the beautiful planet Earth."

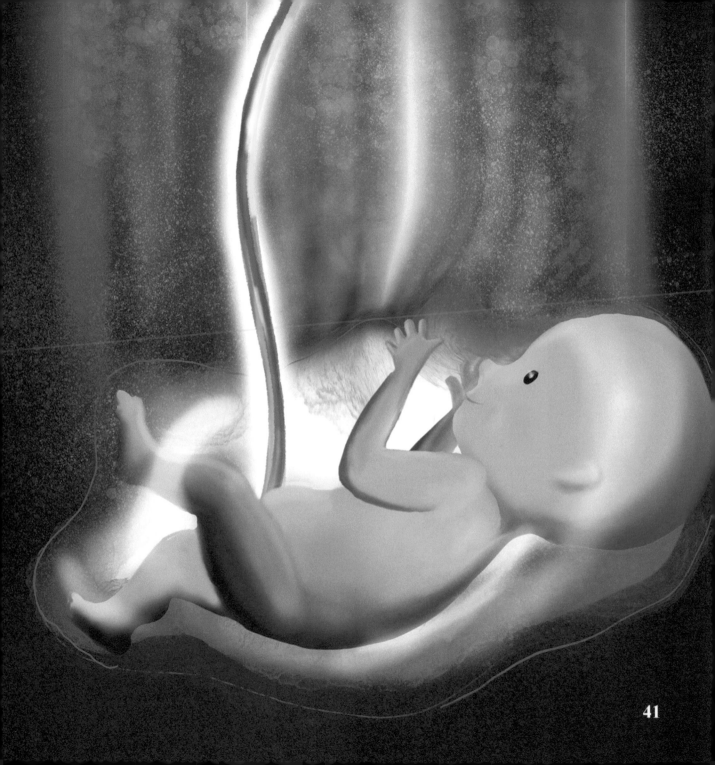

"I will communicate with other Spiritual Beings in physical bodies and co-create with them as we manifest Inspired and Infinite Perfection".

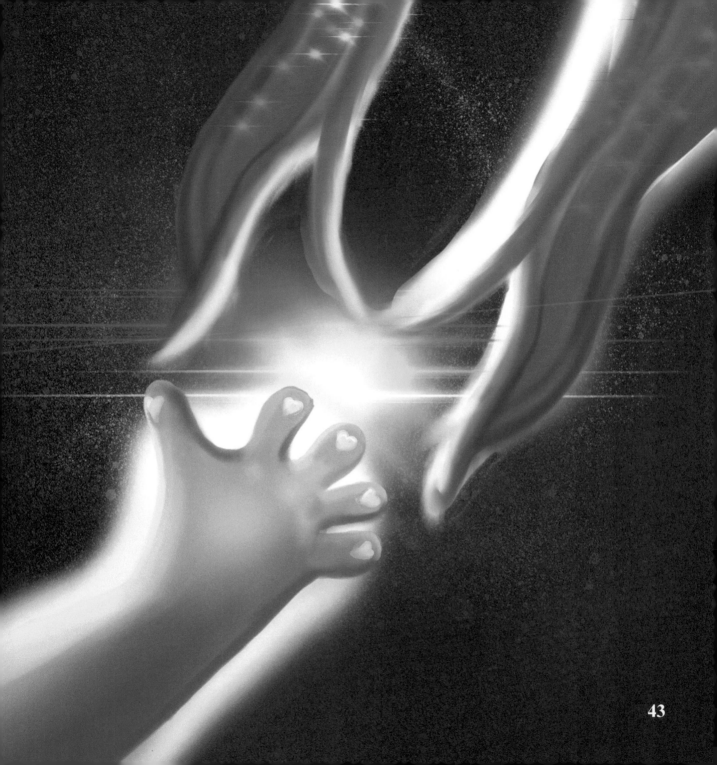

43

"This facet of the Divine Plan for Life is manifesting now, as I see the Heart Flame glowing within the crystalline heart of this Precious Being—the threefold flame of blue, pink and yellow—radiating out into the world the Essence of the best that Life can offer. These are the Power, Love, and Wisdom of the Divine Nature that is inherently theirs."

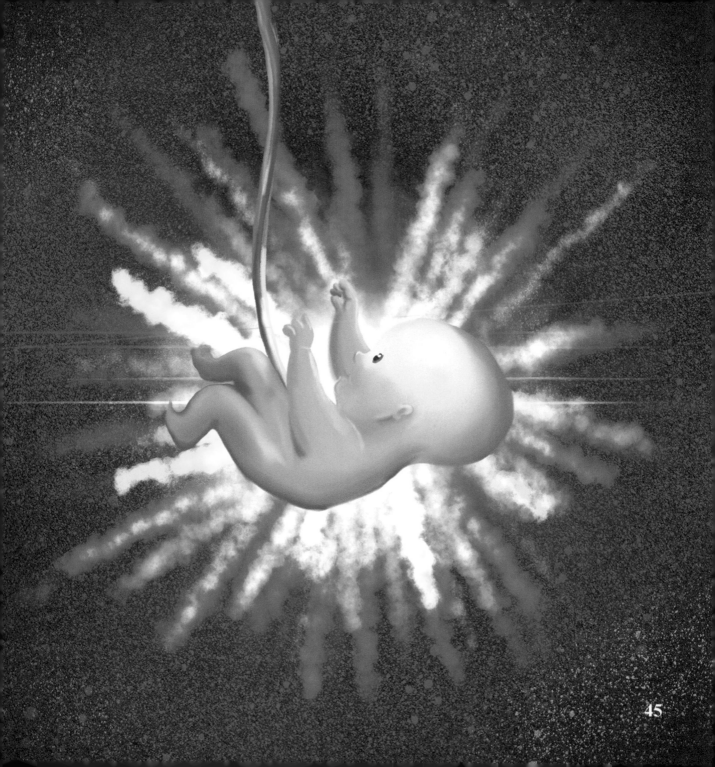

Epilogue

For Parents' Eyes Only

Many fables, fairy tales, and myths throughout the ages have reflected the mysteries of our beginnings. More recently I shared through *The First Fairy Tale: Book I* the miracle of conception and then, in *The First Fairy Tale: Book II*, the initial awakening of our hearts. Both of these stories represent an ideal. These tales are designed for babies and children to hear at a deep level of mind that can comprehend the miraculous unfolding of Life itself without finding fault or becoming overwhelmed with scientific descriptions. Indeed, children have not yet matured to the point that their conscious minds can think through complex explanations.

Here we share the exquisite development that takes place during the remainder of the 280 days prior to birth. Described in this epilogue is more detail about the process of gestation that encompasses the greatest period of development that human beings ever experience. It is directed by a wisdom beyond our comprehension. How does each cell know what it is to do and where to locate among the trillions of cells assembling the body of a new human being?

According to conventional wisdom, as the heart forms, three layers of cells are developing: the ectoderm, endoderm and mesoderm. The ectoderm astonishingly separates into the brain and nervous system as well as the skin that covers the body. The skin will provide tactile sensations to the brain, which will be enclosed in the darkness of the cranium. The brain has a voracious appetite for sensory data. The endoderm will develop into the lining of the gastrointestinal tract, the liver, pancreas and thyroid. The mesoderm will become skeleton, connective tissues, blood and urogenital systems, and muscle tissue.

All this is occurring within a tiny body less than a quarter inch long! By the fifth week chambers have formed within the heart while arm and leg buds appear externally. Primitive air passages that evolve into lungs, and other internal organs begin to take shape. The umbilical cord begins to protrude and eyes and nostrils start to appear. Electrical activity in the brain can be measured this early! This Little One is even reacting to hair-fine stimulation with sensitivity to touch.

By six weeks the rapid growth includes eyelids, the tip of the nose, and both internal and external portions of the ears. The arms extend forward displaying elbows and little digital rays emanate from their ends that will become fingers. The main divisions of the central nervous system have been established including the spinal cord, hind brain, midbrain and forebrain. This precious being is still less than an inch in length. In another week and at just over an inch in size, hands, feet, fingers and toes have emerged and hands meet over the heart. Self-initiated movement is beginning, and head and neck are distinguished from one another.

At nine weeks, the head is almost half the baby's total length of about two inches. The end of the tenth week signals the shift from the embryonic period of the baby's life to the fetal period. The earlier period is more fraught with peril; now, within the fetus, organ systems are well under development and growth continues apace. External genitalia begin to show but male and female identities are not established for another three weeks. The baby's heartbeat can now be heard with the assistance of Doppler technology.

Between the seventh and eleventh weeks the fetus has doubled in length and can measure three inches. The head, about half the size of the body's length, will be only one third in comparison to the body by week 21, and at birth only about one fourth the body's size. Facial features align and male and female genitalia are more distinguishable during the eleventh and twelfth weeks.

Now over four inches long, the fetus is covered with fine hair and eyes and ears continue to develop. All systems are GO, and between weeks 16 and 20, mommies begin to feel their babies move! This is called quickening. During this time the baby has begun to hear, has developed taste buds, and can sense temperature changes. Eventually, all the baby's senses will provide the hidden brain with rich information which creates perceptions of the world, distinguishes differences, makes decisions, and appreciates life based on experiences being recorded at a cellular level.

Babies can swallow amniotic fluid by week 21, helping the development of the digestive system. Baby is getting plumper; by week 22 baby can weigh over a pound. Babies born too early, at 23 weeks, have been known to survive, but the best place to grow is in mother's body.

Books, videos, you tube presentations, and websites now abound to describe week by week your baby's development in the womb. Beyond the first 70 days, or one quarter of the way through the ideal 280 days of pregnancy, your baby's systems are all fully on line and maturing—they were formed in the first quarter. Baby is getting bigger until it no longer fits comfortably in the womb and must exit. Soon baby will be in your arms, looking into your eyes, recognizing your scent, hearing your voice without fluid filling its ears, and being soothed by your touch.

Lightning Source UK Ltd.
Milton Keynes UK
UKHW050503080223
416583UK00003B/126